THE FOREVER
CHRISTMAS
TREE

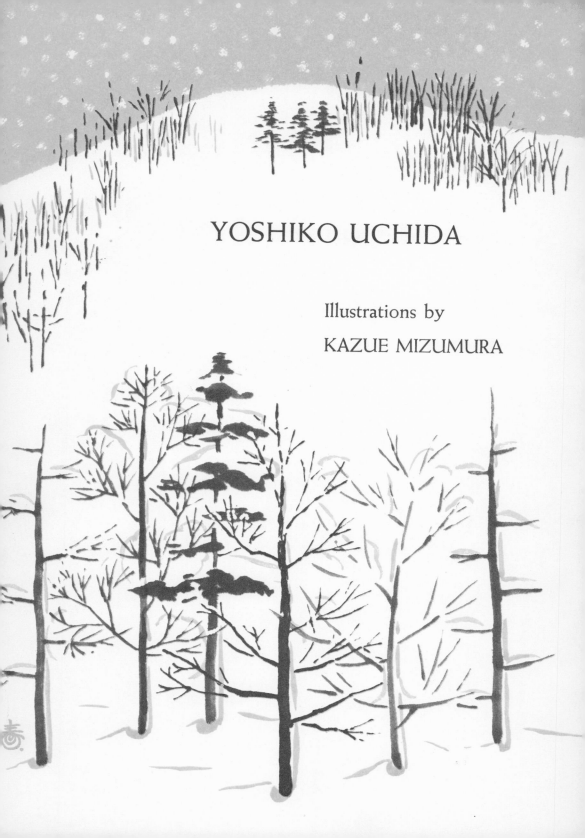

YOSHIKO UCHIDA

Illustrations by
KAZUE MIZUMURA

THE FOREVER

CHRISTMAS TREE

Charles Scribner's Sons, New York

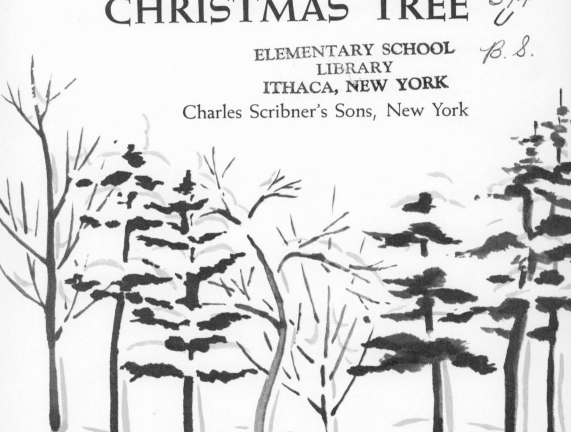

In memory of

Tonton

who might have been

the Old Man

It was December in Sugi Village high in the hills of
Japan. Already the first snow had covered the land, and
the fields looked cold and bleak. Now the days were
short and the nights were long, and it was the quiet time
of the year.

It was also a lonely time, especially for a little boy named Takashi who lived at the edge of the village. There were no more persimmons for him to pick or mushrooms to hunt in the dark secret places of the pine woods. The north wind shivered through the bamboo grove where he liked to play, and it became a forlorn place, too cold even for fighting shadow dragons with bamboo swords. There was nothing at all to do now but wait for the New Year, and that seemed very far away.

If only something wonderfully special and exciting would happen, Takashi thought. But in the quiet village, one day was much like every other. Takashi awakened each morning to the sounds of Mother cooking rice and bean soup in the kitchen. Soon after, Father went to work in the fields, and his sister Kaya, who was eight, went off to school. Mother was always busy with her chores and there was no one to play with except his dog Shiro. On very cold days, however, Shiro would curl up in some dark corner and go to sleep. Then there was no one at all.

If only I had someone to play with, Takashi thought. If only I had a friend next door.

Their only neighbor, however, was an old man whose name was Mr. Toda and who seemed as old as forever. His face was covered with wrinkles, and he had a long thin beard as white as an egret's breast. Whenever Takashi saw him, he looked as gloomy as a thunderstorm, so at home Takashi always called him Mr. Thunder.

Mr. Toda did not have any friends either. He thought people were a great bother so he lived all alone, reading his books and tending his garden.

Deep down in his heart, however, Mr. Toda longed for a friend to talk with during the lonely days of his old age. Then too, there was the big worry that hung about his head like a heavy stone. Who would think of him when he was gone? Who would burn incense at his grave and leave him flowers and sweet cakes? There was no one. This worried Mr. Toda and made him sad. And because he was sad, he looked more than ever like a thunderstorm.

Mr. Toda knew, of course, that there was a little boy named Takashi next door. But he had no time for little boys. They paddled in puddles, carried toads in their pockets, stole his persimmons and trampled on his onions and cabbages. In short, little boys were a nuisance, and he had put up a tall hedge around his garden to keep them all out. Takashi stayed as far away from Mr. Toda's hedge as he possibly could.

One day a cold and fierce wind blew from the icy mountains, and hundreds of snowflakes sifted down from the skies, covering the village with still another layer of whiteness. The snow covered Mr. Toda's roof, and it covered the thatch over Takashi's little house.

It was too cold to play outside, so Takashi sat where he could watch the road. He waited and waited for Kaya to come home from school. When at last he saw her, she was running, and Takashi knew she had something special to tell. As soon as she was in the house, the words came tumbling out.

"Today we learned about Christmas!" she said, and the bright glow of her excitement quickly spilled out to fill Takashi too.

Takashi did not know much about Christmas for no one celebrated it in Sugi Village. It was the New Year that mattered.

Kaya pulled Takashi toward the *kotatsu*, and they sat warming their feet at the container of charcoal as she told him all that she had learned. She told him about the very first Christmas in Bethlehem, and she told about the wisemen and the shepherds who traveled over barren hills and fields to see the baby Jesus. Then at the very last, she told him about Christmas trees with their lights and colored balls and strings of popcorn and candy.

Takashi listened with his eyes wide open. He listened hard, with his whole body. When Kaya finished, he closed his eyes, and he could see a Christmas tree all covered with candy and lights and colored balls. It was a wonderful thing to think about. It was like a shining pearl to hold in his hand, to be looked at and thought about in the secret darkness of night. From that moment Takashi wanted a Christmas tree of his own more than anything else.

The next day Takashi went outside with Shiro and looked at the trees around their house. There were gnarled pine trees that looked like old men with bent backs. There were pine trees that soared higher than the village fire tower. There were leafy trees and barren trees that danced with the wind, but none that looked anything at all like a Christmas tree.

Just when Takashi thought he would never ever find
a Christmas tree, Shiro did something to help him. He
saw a rabbit run through the vegetable patch. He wriggled his nose, pointed his tail and bounded away after

it. Then he slithered under the hedge and ran right into
Mr. Toda's yard.

"Come back!" Takashi shouted. "Stop!"

But Shiro did not listen when there were rabbits to be
chased.

Old Mr. Thunder would beat Shiro with a stick if he caught him, Takashi thought. He ran to the hedge and got down flat on his stomach. He scrunched up his face and peered through the hole that Shiro had wriggled through. The yard was empty! The old man was nowhere in sight and neither was Shiro. Takashi sighed with relief and was about to get up when he saw a beautiful little fir tree planted in a wooden tub. The wind had knocked it over, and the tree was crooked and askew. But even so Takashi could tell that it was a perfect Christmas tree.

All it needed were some trimmings. If only he could have that tree!

Takashi told Kaya about the little fir tree in Mr. Toda's yard.

"Help me," he said to her. "I want it for a Christmas tree."

So Kaya thought. She thought and she thought. She tugged at her short black hair as though she might pull a wonderful idea from her head. But nothing came.

"Surely we cannot have the old man's tree," she said, "but let's make some decorations anyway. We can hang them on the branches of our pine tree."

Kaya got out scissors and paste, and from her special hiding place she brought her box of papers. Here she kept ribbons, string, tinfoil and pieces of colored paper that had once wrapped a sweet bean paste cake or had been on a can of dried seaweed. She called it her "Precious Paper Box" and this was the first time in all of Takashi's life that he had been allowed to have something from it. At the very bottom Kaya had a brand new package of colored paper that she had been saving for just such an occasion as this.

Together they cut and pasted. They made many, many loops and linked them together in one long chain. They folded golden storks and silver balloons. They made boats and birds and flowers and baskets from all sorts of lovely colored squares of paper. Then they put them all away carefully in two big boxes.

"On the day that is called Christmas Eve," Kaya said, "we can hang these on our pine tree."

Takashi nodded, but he was thinking how much better they would look on the old man's little fir tree. He thought about the tree as he ate his supper that night. He thought about it as the family sat close around the warmth of the charcoal in the *kotatsu*.

"Takashi is quiet tonight," his father said.

"His head is full of many things," his mother answered gently.

Kaya nodded. "I know," she said. "His head is full of Christmas."

And because she was still so full of Christmas herself, she told her mother and father all that she had told Takashi.

Her father listened as he smoked his pipe. Her mother listened as she mended an apron.

"Ah," she said smiling, "Christmas has the sound of happiness in it."

Father nodded. "It is like a candle on a dark night," he said.

"No, no," Takashi said. "It is like a fir tree full of colored trimmings. That is Christmas."

That night, as he lay on his quilts, Takashi closed his eyes and saw his Christmas tree. It was Mr. Toda's fir tree covered with the colored balls and flowers and chains that he had made with Kaya. And as he slept, he dreamed that the old man gave him the tree to be his very own.

Early the next morning Takashi crept softly to the

hedge. He made sure Mr. Toda was not about, and then
he looked for the fir tree. But the tree was not where it
had been before. The old man had planted it beside his
front entrance, and now it would stand there sturdy and
firm forever. Takashi hung his head. He could no longer
even dream about having the tree.

On December twenty-fourth Kaya came home rosy cheeked from the cold and the excitement that bubbled inside her.

"Today is the day that is called Christmas Eve," she said to Takashi. "Tonight we will decorate our pine tree."

"Are you really going out on such a cold night to trim the tree?" Mother asked them after supper.

The children nodded. "We have to have a Christmas tree," Takashi answered.

"And we have the trimmings all ready," Kaya explained.

"Dress warmly then," Mother said.

"Take care not to slip on the snow," Father warned.

Kaya and Takashi bundled themselves up and carried out the boxes of decorations. They went to the foot of the pine tree and looked up at it. Then Kaya looked inside each box.

"We have only enough decorations for one branch of this big tree," she said sadly.

Takashi nodded. "Maybe we could trim the persimmon tree instead," he said. "We have enough for that little tree."

But the persimmon tree was bare, with not a single leaf on it. It simply would not do for a Christmas tree.

Kaya and Takashi stood for a moment in the icy coldness of the winter night. The sky was black except for the tiny stars that shone like faraway icicles. Takashi blew out his breath and saw the mist of its warmth in the air.

Then, without saying anything to each other, Kaya and Takashi began to walk in the same direction. They moved closer and closer to the hedge that enclosed Mr. Toda's garden. All the lights in his house were out, for the old man went to bed early when it was cold.

"Shall we just see how it looks?" Kaya asked. "Just for a minute?"

Takashi knew what she meant. It was what he wanted to do too. Together they hurried in the darkness toward the old man's fir tree, walking carefully so they would not slip and drop their boxes of trimmings.

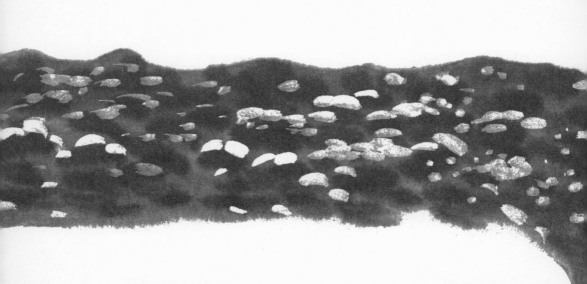

Then silently, without a word, they took out their colored paper trimmings and decorated the little tree. They looped the paper chains around its branches, and they hung the golden birds and baskets. There were just enough decorations to trim the whole tree. Then they stepped back to look at it.

"Oh," Takashi said, "it is a real Christmas tree!"

Kaya clasped her hands together and said, "It is the most beautiful Christmas tree in the whole wide world."

62641

Even after many minutes they still could not make themselves take down the trimmings.

Takashi spoke in a whisper. "Do you think Mr. Thunder would be mad if we left it just for one day? So we can see it in the daytime and show Mother and Father?"

Kaya thought for a moment and then she smiled. "I do not think he will be angry, Takashi," she said. "Maybe...maybe...if he can be filled with Christmas too, he will even like it just a little."

So they took one last look and then ran, stumbling and tumbling in their hurry to get home.

That night, as they went to sleep, they lay on their quilts wondering in the darkness. Would the old man be terribly angry?

Early the next morning Takashi woke up thinking about his Christmas tree. And in the house next door Mr. Toda was up before the sun. He drank some tea and ate some pickles with his rice. Then he wrapped a wool scarf about his throat, put on a warm coat over his *kimono* and slipped on his wooden clogs to go outside. He slid open the door and blinked at the sun as it climbed over the top of the hill. It made brilliant patterns of light on the snow, and the old man blinked again. Even his little fir tree seemed covered with bright colors. He stepped closer and bent to inspect it.

At that moment Takashi came to look at the tree, for he could not wait a moment longer to see it once more. He peered carefully from behind the hedge and suddenly he was looking right at Mr. Thunder himself.

"Come here," the old man beckoned.

Takashi felt as though all his bones had melted. He could not move or say a word.

"Come here, child," the old man said again. "Do you know who did this to my tree?"

At last Takashi nodded. "I...I...I...did," he said in a small voice. "Kaya and I did it. It's...it's a Christmas tree."

And then, still keeping a safe distance away so he could run quickly if necessary, Takashi told the old man how they had trimmed the tree the night before.

"Ah," Mr. Toda said slowly. He had heard of Christmas, and he knew about Christmas trees. He tugged at his white beard as he searched for the right words.

Takashi was so frightened, he was ready to run home. But as he turned to go he bumped into Kaya who had come with Mother and Father. They all bowed to the old man.

"I am sorry our children trimmed your tree without permission," Father said solemnly.

"They should have spoken to you first," Mother added. "I hope they did no harm."

But even as they spoke they had to smile, for the Christmas tree looked so bright and cheerful standing in the snow.

The old man nodded as though he agreed with every word they said. Then slowly, the crooked curve of a smile crept over his face.

"It is the first time in my life that I have had a Christmas tree," he said.

"Then you are not angry?" Kaya asked.

The old man shook his head. "You have not harmed the tree," he answered.

Takashi had to ask too. "You're not angry?" he repeated and forgetting that he was really talking to Mr. Toda, he called him Mr. Thunder right to his face. Still the old man did not get angry.

"Would it be all right if I showed my friends?" Kaya asked. Without waiting for an answer, she ran off down the road toward the village. Takashi did not want to miss a minute of the excitement. Quickly he ran after Kaya shouting, "Wait for me!" He followed her as she ran from house to house, calling to all her friends.

"Come see!" she called. "Come see our Christmas tree." Takashi shouted like an echo, "Come see! Come see!"

Together they ran and ran into the face of the icy wind, and they did not even feel the cold.

Big children and small children, boys and girls came from all over the village to see the tree. There were even some babies carried on their big sisters' backs. And some of the boys carried pet toads in their pockets. They all stood in the old man's yard and trampled on the onions and spinach planted beneath the snow.

At first the old man didn't know what to say or do. He had never seen so many children all at once.

"Get off my onions," he said in a small voice, but no one heard him at all.

When he saw how excited and happy the children were, he could scowl no longer. He went into the house, opened his cupboard and found a package of rice crackers. There were just enough crackers for everyone.

The children looked and looked. They looked at the old man and they looked at the tree, for both of them were new and wonderful sights to see. They sniffed and rubbed their noses, and they ate their rice crackers. Everyone felt good inside, even the old man. He turned to Takashi and said, "You may trim the tree next year too."

"And the year after that?" Takashi asked.

The old man nodded. "Every Christmastime," he said.

"Forever?" Takashi asked.

The old man nodded again. "For as long as you like."

A real fir tree to trim every Christmas! His own beautiful Christmas tree! Takashi thought he would burst with joy. He jumped and hopped about in the garden, and Shiro ran in eager circles around him, churning up the snow and squashing onions everywhere.

"Old man, you are not so grumpy after all!" Takashi said.

Gradually, one by one, everyone went home. But Takashi and Kaya could not stay away for very long. They ran home for a while and then came back again and again to put another silver stork or a new chain of colored loops on the tree. Finally, they added a star of gold to the tip of their beautiful tree. Now it was complete.

The old man came to watch the children for he, too, found it hard to stay away from the tree. And as he watched, he knew that for the first time in many, many months, he was no longer worried or sad. He knew that he had not only found Christmas, but a great deal more.

"Come, Takashi," Kaya said at last. "We must go home now."

Takashi blew at his icy cold fingers and took one more look at the tree.

"Our forever Christmas tree!" he said happily.

Then he waved to Mr. Toda and the old man raised his hand in return.

As Takashi walked home, crunching over the icy snow, a grin spread slowly over his face, for suddenly he realized that at last something wonderful and exciting had happened to him right in Sugi Village. He had discovered Christmas and he had found a new friend next door. He had waited a long, long time, but in the last days of the twelfth month, this year had become a very special one indeed.